THE(

FL

NOTEBOOK FOR MINECRAFT FANS

Property of:

Bibliografische Information der Deutschen Nationalbibliothek:
Die Deutsche Nationalbibliothek verzeichnet diese Publikation in der Deutschen Nationalbibliografie; detaillierte bibliografische Daten sind im Internet über http://dnb.dnb.de abrufbar.

© 2016 Theo von Taane; 1. Auflage

Texte und Illustrationen: **Theo von Taane**

Herstellung und Verlag: BoD – Books on Demand, Norderstedt

ISBN: 9783743154186

More books of Theo von Taane

book	ISBN / order nr.
FUNCRAFT - Math Coloring Book Minecraft Minis	9783741281952
FUNCRAFT - Math Coloring Book Superheroes in Minecraft	9783741289972
FUNCRAFT - Math Coloring Book for Minecraft Fans	9783741292682
FUNCRAFT - Enderdragon Notebook for Minecraft Fans	9783743154148
FUNCRAFT - Notebook for Minecraft Fans	9783743154186
FUNCRAFT - Merry Christmas to all Minecraft Fans! (Notebook)	9783743163348
FUNCRAFT - Happy New Year to all Minecraft Fans! (Notebook)	9783743163355
Password Logbook for Minecraft Fans	9783743163386
Pokemon GO - Team Red Notebook	9783741286070
Pokemon GO - Team Blue Notebook	9783741286063
Pokemon GO - Team Yellow Notebook	9783741286049
Pokemon GO - Pikachu Notebook	9783741286087
Majestic Flowers and Butterflies - Adult Coloring Book	9783739227085
Football tacticboard and training workbook	9783734749605
Badminton tacticboard and training workbook	9783734749643
Baseball tacticboard and training workbook	9783734749650
Basketball tacticboard and training workbook	9783734749681
Bowling tacticboard and training workbook	9783734749698
Cricket tacticboard and training workbook	9783734749711
Ice Hockey tacticboard and training workbook	9783734749728
Fencing tacticboard and training workbook	9783734749735
Field Hockey tacticboard and training workbook	9783734749810
Football (Soccer) tacticboard and training workbook	9783734749827
Futsal tacticboard and training workbook	9783734749834
Handball tacticboard and training workbook	9783734749841
Lacrosse Women tacticboard and training workbook	9783734749858
Lacrosse Men tacticboard and training workbook	9783734749865
Netball tacticboard and training workbook	9783734749872
Rugby tacticboard and training workbook	9783734749889
Chess tacticboard and training workbook	9783734749896
Squash tacticboard and training workbook	9783734749902
Tennis tacticboard and training workbook	9783734749919
Table Tennis tacticboard and training workbook	9783734749926
Volleyball tacticboard and training workbook	9783734749933
Water Polo tacticboard and training workbook	9783734749940

...futher titles available and in preparation.

CPSIA information can be obtained
at www.ICGtesting.com
Printed in the USA
LVHW020102240920
666973LV00015B/545

9 783743 154186